Grandma Birdie's Red String

written by
amir dekel

illustrated by
sona & jacob

One day when I was playing
with mommy's purse,
I found a little bag
with a mysterious
red string inside.

I wondered what it was...

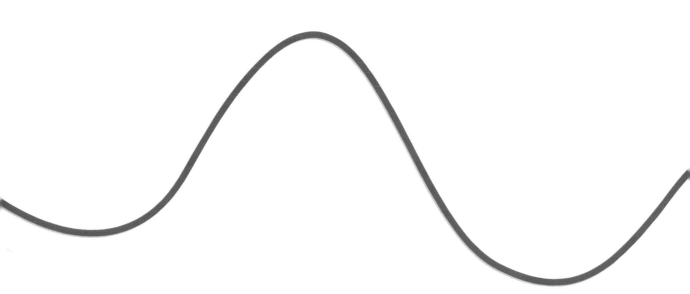

"What is this, mommy?" I asked.

Mommy explained that it used
to belong to Grandma Birdie,
who is her mommy.

I love my Grandma Birdie
very much and I remembered
that when I was just a teeny
tiny baby, she would come
over to our house all the time.

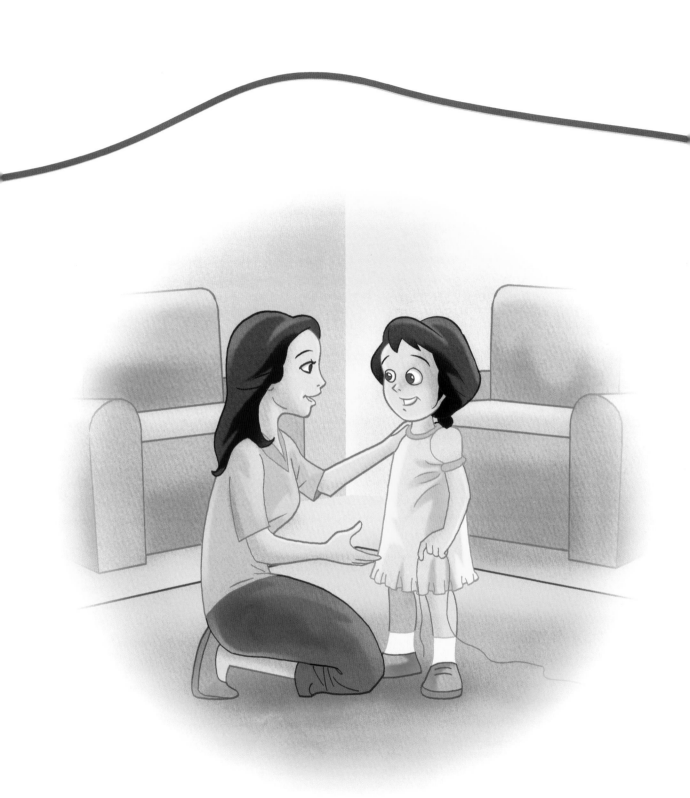

I remember how we would play games and read books together. She would always wear these really big eyeglasses and she cooked delicious food.

Mommy told me there was a very special story about this red string and I couldn't wait to hear it!

"Where did Grandma Birdie get this red string?" I asked.

Mommy said she got it at a magical place that she heard about from her family a long time ago, before I was even born.

Everyone believed that this place had very special powers!

Grandma Birdie walked with the string around this magical place seven times and then she rolled it into a little red ball and put it in her purse.

It sure was a very long string.

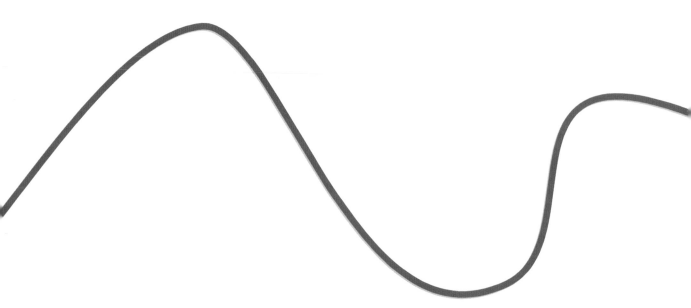

Mommy said that whenever
a new baby was born in the family,
Grandma Birdie would tie little
pieces of the string to the baby's things.

The family would always find
red strings tied to the strollers,
high chairs and car seats.

They sometimes even found
them under the baby cribs.

Grandma Birdie told mommy
that the red string will keep all of us
safe, healthy and happy, forever.

And that's why she made sure
to tie it to all our things.

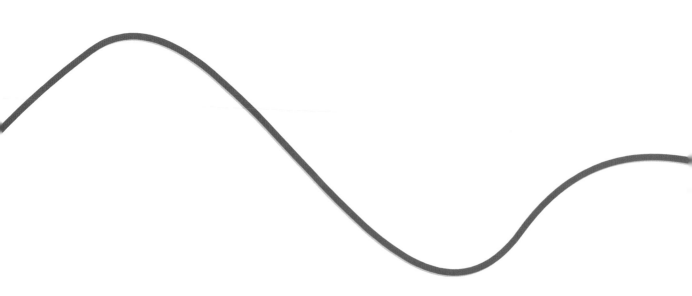

There was still a lot of string left in mommy's purse.

But it really looked like Grandma Birdie used up a lot of it on all her grandchildren.

I even remembered that
she made a little red string
bracelet for every one of us when
we were old enough to wear one.

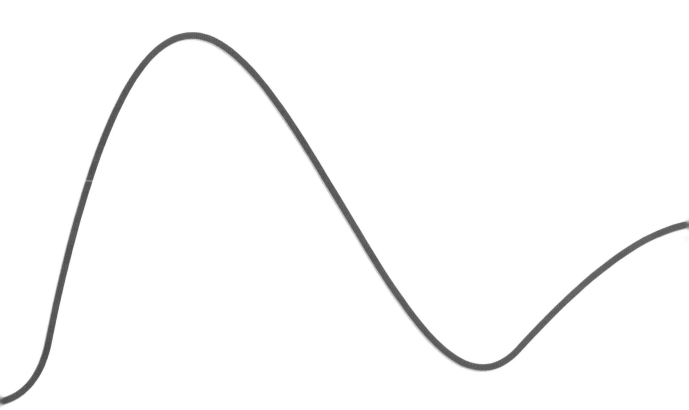

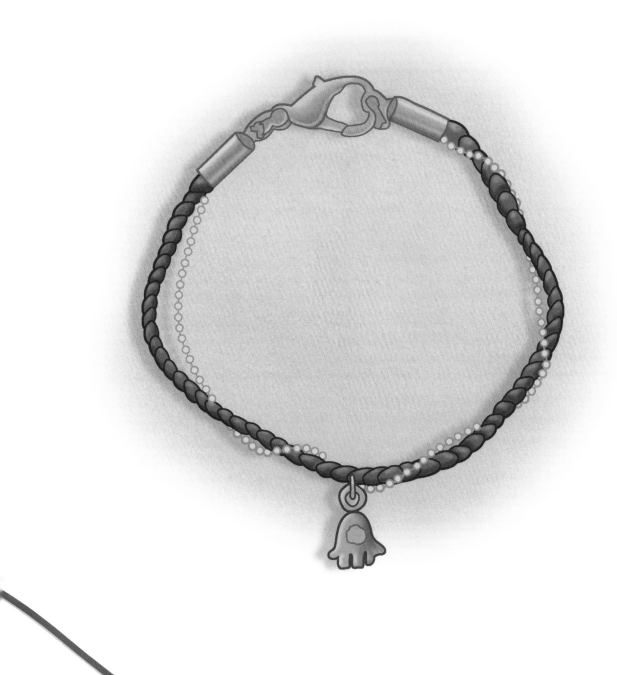

Then one day Grandma Birdie
said she had to give the rest
of her string to someone else.

And guess what?

She decided to give it
to my mommy!

Mommy told me that this way, when we have new babies in the family, she can continue the tradition.

Mommy will use Grandma Birdie's red string just like she did.

"And one day," mommy said,
"I will pass the red string to you."

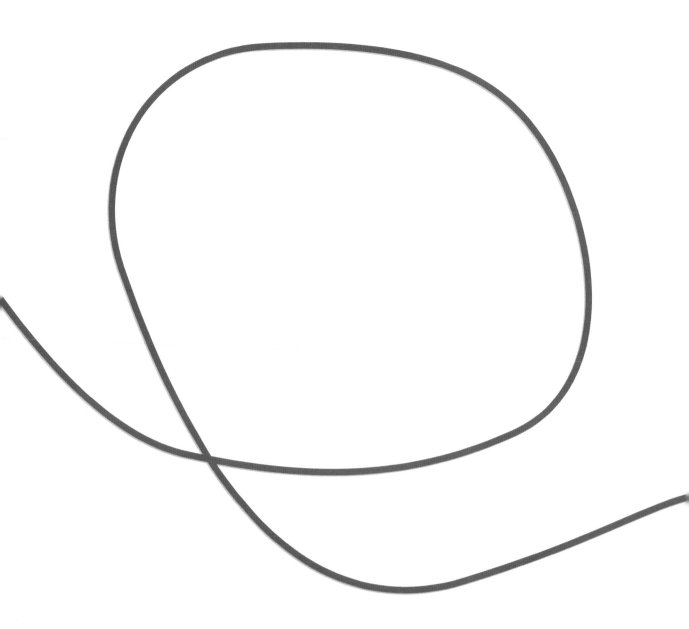

For my daughters,
Kiki & Bella

In memory of
my grandmother,
Zipora Dekel

—A.D.

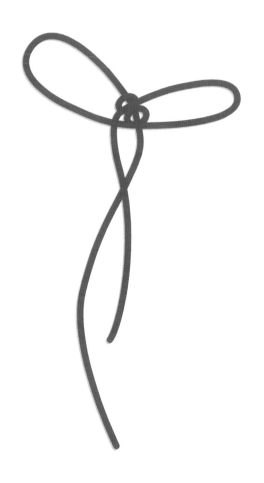

Cover and interior design and layout by Erin Bradley Dangar / www.dangardesign.com

© 2010 by Amir Dekel

Made in the USA
Charleston, SC
08 May 2010